PROFESSIONAL

S•T•Y•L•I•N•G•S

for the
Solo Pianist

By Noreen Sauls

DEDICATIONS

THIS BOOK IS DEDICATED TO:

• My wonderful parents, Norb and Mickey, for passing on to me, and encouraging, the musical tradition.

• My talented husband, Earl (Gandharva), for his total love and support.

• The memory of my brother, Michael, whose musical talent is a daily inspiration to me.

• My teacher Betty, for her caring, musical guidance, and her own lovely piano arrangements.

• Stuart, Becca and Ed, for involving me in this entire facet of my musical career.

• My family, friends, fellow musicians, teachers, and students, for enriching my life and enhancing my musical persona

• Our Creator, for allowing me to be a channel for musical expression.

Table of Contents

A NOTE FROM THE ARRANGER

This book of arrangements is a little different from most. Each piece is accompanied by an original leadsheet and performance tips, to help you get the maximum benefit out of each one. As you learn each arrangement, you will discover concepts you can apply to the creation of your own piano stylings.

Each of these songs is very special to me, and I hope you enjoy the arrangements, as much as I enjoyed writing them for you. Thank you and God Bless . . .

General Playing Tips

- Some of these arrangements are more difficult than others, and will require some practice, depending on your reading ability. Be patient and play them slowly at first . . . hands apart, if necessary. You'll be sounding great in no time!

- Analyze the chord progressions in each arrangement, and look for substitutions and reharmonizations, by comparing with the original leadsheet provided.

- Take the melodic patterns and chord voicings you like in each arrangement and practice them in all keys, for use in other tunes.

- Study the introductions, endings, vamps, fillers and embellishments. Discover how you can incorporate these into your own playing style.

- For the most part, dynamics, articulations and fingerings have been omitted, so you can make your own choices about the interpretation of these arrangements.

Notes on. . .

Frankie and Johnny

This famous old blues tune is done up in a stride piano style. If you can't reach the left hand tenths, simply roll them from bottom to top, catching the lowest note in the pedal. Be sure to pedal cleanly between each harmonic change. Practice this hand alone before adding the right.

Shakes and grace notes appear throughout the piece. These embellishments lend an authentic bluesy sound. If you're having trouble with the shake, practice it very slowly at first, gradually increasing the speed, while maintaining a LOOSE wrist.

At B, the left hand is the same as before, while the right hand is a written solo, containing many elements used in this style. Repeat this chorus as many times as you like, retaining the left hand and improvising your own right hand solo.

The coda features a traditional tag ending. Learn this in all keys for use in other tunes of this style. You can do the same with the introduction and any other patterns that appeal to you. (See how many of these you can find.)

Frankie and Johnny

Traditional

Moderately

1. Frank - ie And John - ny were lov - ers! Oh, Lord - y how they could
2-13. *(See additional lyrics)*

love! They swore to be true to each oth - er, Just as true as the stars a - bove,

He was her man, But he done her wrong.

Additional Lyrics

2. Frankie she was a good woman
As everybody know,
Spent a hundred dollars
Just to buy her man some clothes.
He was her man, but he was doing her wrong.

3. Frankie went down to the corner
Just for a bucket of beer,
Said: "Mr. Bartender
Has my loving Johnny been here?
He was my man, but he's a-doing me wrong."

4. "Now I don't want to tell you no stories
And I don't want to tell you no lies
I saw your man about an hour ago
With a gal named Nellie Bligh
He was your man, but he's a-doing you wrong."

5. Frankie she went down to the hotel
Didn't go there for fun,
Underneath her kimona
She carried a forty-four gun.
He was her man, but he was doing her wrong.

6. Frankie looked over the transom
To see what she could spy,
There sat Johnny on the sofa
Just loving up Nellie Bligh.
He was her man, but he was doing her wrong.

7. Frankie got down from that high stool
She didn't want to see no more;
Rooty-toot-toot three times she shot
Right through that hardwood door.
He was her man, but he was doing her wrong.

8. Now the first time that Frankie shot Johnny
He let out an awful yell,
Second time she shot him
There was a new man's face in hell.
He was her man, but he was doing her wrong.

9. "Oh roll me over easy
Roll me over slow
Roll me over on the right side
For the left side hurts me so."
He was her man, but he was doing her wrong.

10. Sixteen rubber-tired carriages
Sixteen rubber-tired hacks
They take poor Johnny to the graveyard
They ain't gonna bring him back.
He was her man, but he was doing her wrong.

11. Frankie looked out of the jailhouse
To see what she could see,
All she could hear was a two-string bow
Crying nearer my God to thee.
He was her man, but he was doing her wrong.

12. Frankie she said to the sheriff
"What do you reckon they'll do?"
Sheriff he said "Frankie,
It's the electric chair for you."
He was her man, but he was doing her wrong.

13. This story has no moral
This story has no end
This story only goes to show
That there ain't no good in men!
He was her man, but he was doing her wrong.

Frankie and Johnny

Traditional

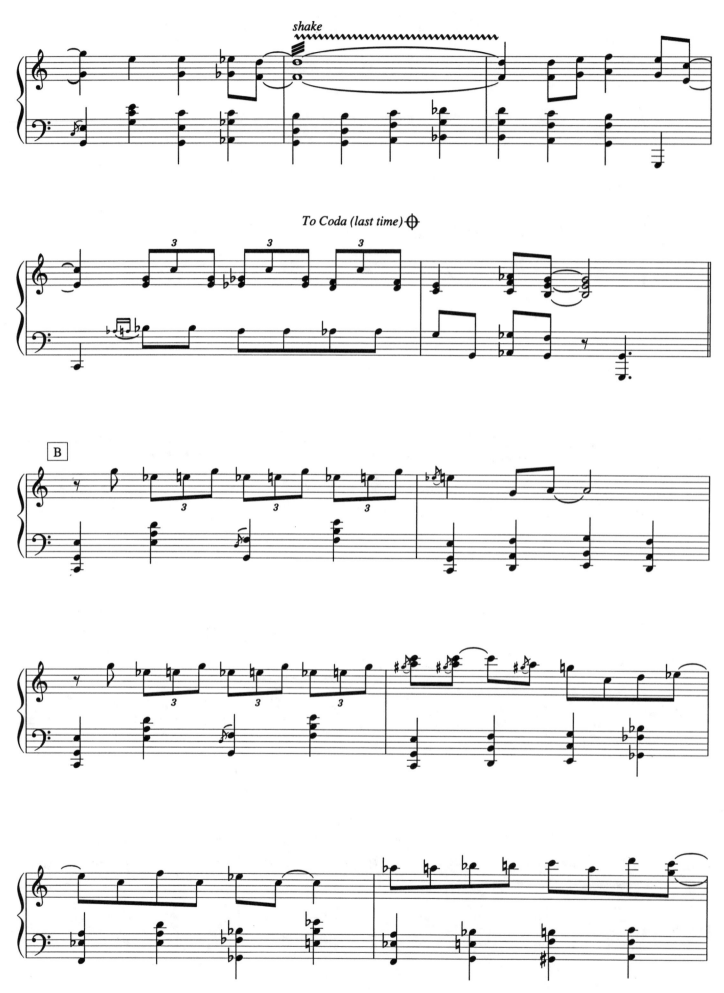

To Coda (last time) ⊕

B

9

Notes on. . .

Amazing Grace

This arrangement opens in a harmonically simple, gospel-like style, featuring grace notes and triplet figures. Take your time in the rubato section, to bring out all of these embellishments and inner voices.

The piece goes into time in measure 11, with a traditional gospel feel. At letter B, a jazz waltz begins, and the harmonies become more complex. To analyze the reharmonization, compare these changes to those in the first chorus. The eighth notes in this section should have a lilting swing feel.

Five measures from the end, the time winds down with a gradual ritard and a return to the gospel style.

Amazing Grace

Traditional

1. A - maz - ing___ Grace! How sweet the
2 - 5. *(See additional lyrics)*

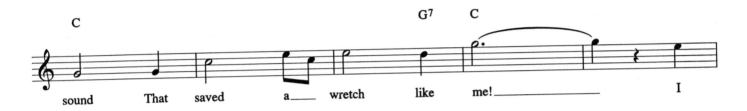

sound That saved a___ wretch like me!___ I

once___ was___ lost but now___ am___ found; Was blind, but___

now I see.___ 'Twas me.___

Additional Lyrics

2. 'Twas grace that taught my heart to fear,
And grace my fears relieved;
How precious did that grace appear
The hour I first believed.

3. Thro' many dangers, toils and snares,
I have already come;
'Tis grace hath bro't me safe thus far,
And grace will lead me home.

4. How sweet the name of Jesus sounds
In a believer's ear.
It soothes his sorrows, heals his wounds,
And drives away his fear.

5. Must Jesus bear the cross alone
And all the world go free?
No, there's a cross for ev'ry one
And there's a cross for me.

Amazing Grace
(for Margabandhu)

John Newton

13

Notes on. . .

Black Is the Color
of My True Love's Hair

This arrangement appears simple, but it is filled with many haunting harmonies. I have always loved old English folk music, and felt the influence of its style while writing this piece.

Most of the voicings are very open, and moving inner voices provide the tension and resolution of various suspensions. Measures 18-21 make use of a left hand B pedal point, with only single notes and/or very simple chords above it. Take plenty of time with the ritard five measures from the end.

The more expression you put into this piece, the more satisfying it will sound. Play the dynamic levels indicated, and then experiment with some of your own. You might even want to add some additional rubato sections.

Saxophonist Johnny Griffin has recorded a lovely version of this tune.

Black Is the Color
of My True Love's Hair

Traditional

Black, black, black is the col - or of my
How I love my_____ love and well she

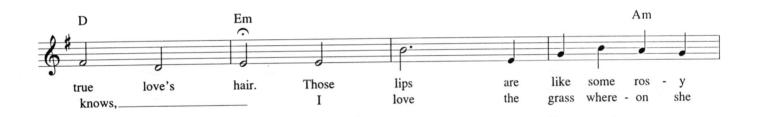

true love's hair. Those lips are like some ros - y
knows,_____ I love the grass where - on she

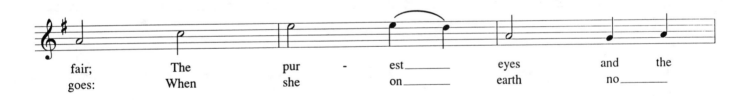

fair; The pur - est_____ eyes and the
goes: When she on_____ earth no_____

neat - est_____ hands, I love the grass where - on she stands.
more__ I_____ see, My life will quick - ly o - ver be.

Black Is the Color of My True Love's Hair

For Gandharva

Traditional

Notes on. . .

Go Down, Moses

This song showed up in one of my early piano books and has always been a special favorite.

The first chorus is from an arrangement I did for my jazz vocal group at William Paterson College. Although written for voices, it sounds well as a piano arrangement, because I tend to write things more pianistically (or sometimes from a big band concept).

Measures 17 and 18 are a transition into an eight measure vamp, that sets up a jazz waltz. (The voicings are like those in John Coltrane's recording of "My Favorite Things.")

The melody re-enters at measure 27. This second chorus will provide you with ideas for incorporating the jazz waltz technique into your own playing. Compare the chord changes with the original leadsheet, to find all the substitutions and reharmonizations.

The second chorus is extended by a tag ending, beginning at measure 51. Analyze the chord changes in this section, practice the progression in all keys and adapt it for use in other tunes.

Go Down, Moses

Traditional

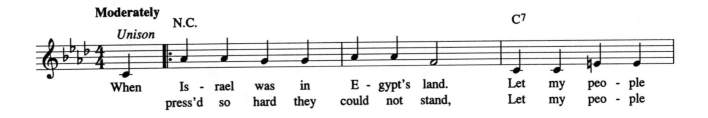

When Is - rael was in E - gypt's land. Let my peo - ple
press'd so hard they could not stand, Let my peo - ple

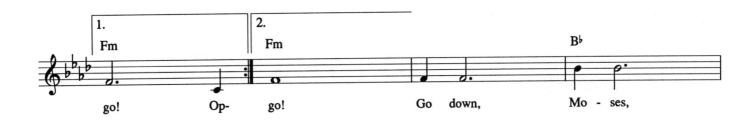

go! Op- go! Go down, Mo - ses,

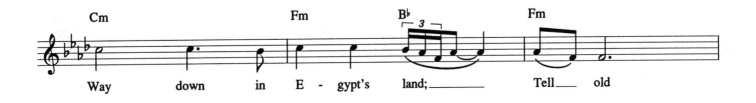

Way down in E - gypt's land;_____ Tell___ old

Pha - roah, Let my peo - ple go!

Go Down, Moses

Traditional

Let my peo - ple go.

Jazz waltz

23

Notes on. . .

Golden Earrings

This tune first came to my attention via a Willie Nelson recording. Jazz players have also taken their turn at it; among them, pianists Keith Jarrett and Geoff Keezer.

The arrangement is in a bossa nova style, but I often play this tune as a jazz waltz. (See if you can convert it yourself, after learning the piece.) It is excellent practice to play tunes in a variety of styles and tempos. Some tunes sound well in more than one setting, and others do not, but you're sure to make some interesting discoveries.

The introduction to this tune is a four-measure vamp, based on a syncopated left hand figure that I must give my bassist-husband the credit for. We actually use it on another Latin tune, in a different key . . . you can do the same. (By the way, the eighth notes are played "straight" in this piece . . .)

The first two measures at A^1 feature a modified left hand figure, with the right hand voiced in fourths. The left hand continues its rhythmic activity throughout most of the arrangement.

At A^2, the left hand begins with fifths and rootless voicings in fourths, for an open sound. This section is harmonized differently from A^1 and A^3 . . . . remember to compare them.

At B (the bridge), measures 1 and 2 and 5 and 6 are sequential in nature. Practice this pattern in other keys, until you feel comfortable, then harmonize other melodic lines that fit this disguised ii-V-I progression.

Three measures from the end, a bluesy quality is introduced in the right hand, grace note-embellished line. The opening vamp then returns for a fade-out ending. Do some improvising in this section.

Golden Earrings

Jay Livingston, Ray Evans
and Victor Young

Golden Earrings

Jay Livingston, Ray Evans
and Victor Young

♩ = 90   Bossa nova
Intro *(repeat as desired)*

A1

Repeat and fade for ending

Fine

Notes on. . .

The Happy Farmer

This piece was one of the first piano duets I ever played, as a young student.

The arrangement begins with blues-like voicings in the first four measures. They are similar to the voicings used in the Miles Davis recording "Freddie The Freeloader" on the album *Kind of Blue*. In measures 9-12, 9ths and 13ths have been added for a fuller sound.

The device used in measure 16 is one that should be learned in all keys. The measure begins on a D chord and ends on D/F#. Passing chords C/E and F#° have been inserted between to create movement and variety.

A left hand D pedal point predominates in measures 17-20, with triadic harmonies above it.

Measures 23-24 are an example of parallel voicings. Every note in the phrase has been voiced in the same way. The minor seconds in the left hand create a colorful dissonance. Omit the 2nd note from the bottom and play the phrase again, to compare the sound.

Examples of ii-V chord movement can be found in measures 14 and 29-30.

The moving left hand figures in measures 35-36 and 39 should be played with "straight" eighth notes. This sets up the ritard which follows. The last four measures are a tag ending, beginning on F7, and moving up chromatically until the resolution in the home key of G.

The Happy Farmer

Robert Schumann

The Happy Farmer

Robert Schumann

Light and lively

rit. to end

Notes on. . .

Greensleeves

Most jazz fans associate this tune with John Coltrane's famous recording from the '60s. If you haven't experienced it, don't wait another minute!!

The first part of this arrangement is centered around arpeggiated left harmonies. Practice this part alone first, working out fingerings, as necessary, to maintain a smooth, flowing line. The eighth notes should be played "straight."

In measure 7, the right hand is harmonized in sixths, continuing through the first chorus. Measure 19 introduces a time change to 3/4 and a jazz waltz feel. The transition is easy to make. (The eighth note in 6/8 equals the quarter note in 3/4.) Compare the two different "feels" and note the contrast between the "straight" and "swing" rhythms.

Six measures from the end, the "straight" eighth feeling returns, even though the tune remains in 3/4. A gradual ritard brings the tune to its end.

Greensleeves

Traditional

Additional Lyrics

2. I have been ready at your hand,
   To grant whatever you would crave;
   I have both wagered life and land,
   Your love and good-will for to have.
   If you intend thus to disdain,
   It does the more enrapture me,
   And even so, I still remain
   A lover in captivity.

3. My men were clothed all in green,
   And they did ever wait on thee;
   All this was gallant to be seen;
   And yet thou wouldst not love me.
   Thou couldst desire no earthly thing
   But still thou hadst it readily.
   Thy music still to play and sing;
   And yet thou wouldst not love me.

4. Well, I will pray to God on high,
   That thou my constancy mayst see,
   And that yet once before I die,
   Thou wilt vouchsafe to love me.
   Ah, Greensleeves, now farewell, adieu,
   To God I pray to prosper thee,
   For I am still thy lover true,
   Come once again and love me.

Greensleeves

Traditional

Jazz waltz

39

Notes on. . .

Harlem Nocturne

This piece incorporates melodic and rhythmic ideas from blues and boogie-woogie styles. The foundation is provided by the bass line, established in the four measure introduction. At A^2 it is embellished by the addition of a triplet figure on beat 4.

One measure before B is an example of chromatic voicings . . . in this case, dominant 7ths with an added 13th. Practice this (and all voicings) in every key, up and down the keyboard.

At B, the bass line expands to all triplet figures, with blues/boogie elements. Measures 7 and 8 of B feature sequential chord voicings descending in whole steps. Look for other parallel voicings in the piece.

The last two measures return to the original vamp. Use this section to explore some of your own improvised lines, in the right hand. Then improvise a new bass line!!

Harlem Nocturne

Dick Rogers
and Earle Hagen

Harlem Nocturne

Dick Rogers and Earle Hagen

To Coda $\oplus$

43

A²

D.S. 𝄋 al Coda

⊕ Coda

Repeat and fade to end

Notes on. . .

Just a Closer Walk with Thee

This traditional hymn begins with simple harmonies. Note the movement of the "tenor" voice in the first measure, and the "alto" and "bass" voices in measure 4. These lines complement the slower moving melody.

In measures 5-8 there is a left hand G pedal point supporting the melody, which is harmonized in triads. In measures 10-11, sixths are used for harmonization.

In the second chorus, the tune expands to a broader reharmonization, including more extended chord voicings. Compare them to the original version.

The final chord contains six notes in the right hand. Play the bottom two with your thumb.

Just a Closer Walk with Thee

Traditional

Just a Closer Walk with Thee

Traditional

Notes on. . .

Largo

This arrangement is adapted from a big band chart I wrote last year. Of all the pieces in the book, this one is the least "jazzed up." Despite my experimentation with different reharmonizations, and finding many suitable ones, I kept coming back to this setting, and decided to "let well enough alone." Simple harmonies can be very beautiful and effective and we shouldn't forget them because we're playing jazz.

Note how the melody is harmonized throughout, with sixths (measures 9 and 10), thirds underneath (13 and 14), and in full chords with octave doublings (15 and 16).

Measures 17-19 utilize a left hand G pedal point, with the harmonies moving above it. Make up your own exercise, by selecting various bass notes as a pedal point and playing different chords above it.

Measures 20-22 feature rolled chords in both hands. (Begin the roll at the same time in both hands).

Largo

Antonin Dvořák

*(Dedicated to Florice Whyte Kovan
and Virgil Whyte's All Girl Band)*

Largo

(from "New World Symphony")

Antonin Dvořák

53

Notes on. . .

Liebesträum

An eight measure introduction, with a left hand G pedal point, sets up a jazz waltz version of this popular Franz Liszt composition. Study the rhythmic figures and the interaction between the two hands, and use these as a guide for playing other tunes in this style.

All three A sections have been harmonized in a different way. Be sure to analyze and compare them.

Note the use of pedal points and sequences in letter B. The last seven measures are marked by a ritard, which progresses gradually to the tune's end. The eighth notes in the final three measures should be played "straight," as opposed to those in the rest of the piece.

The final chord, G-flat MAJ.7 (9, ♯11, 13) (OR A-flat/G-flat MAJ.7), is the flat 5 of the home key (C). Try this technique to end other tunes in your repertoire.

Liebesträum

Franz Lizst

Liebesträum

Franz Liszt

Notes on. . .

Memories of You

This has always been one of my favorite tunes, so I've done a lot of experimenting with it.

The introduction has a sequential-type pattern, based on a melodic fragment from measures 5 and 6. Each measure outlines a ii-V progression.

The 3rd measure of A^1 is an example of "block chords," a style made popular by pianist George Shearing. The melody is doubled at the octave with the harmonies filled out in between. It is a refreshing change of sound and texture. First, practice this technique by harmonizing scales. When you feel comfortable with it, play an entire tune that way. A simple ballad is best to begin with.

The filler one measure before A^2 consists of chromatically descending 7ths in the left hand. At A^2, a stride pattern takes over the left hand for 6 measures, with various fillers in the right hand. Note the use of octaves here.

The first 2 measures of B (the bridge) also involve octaves, with one note taken by each hand, creating a texture change. This effective technique can be used in your improvisations as well.

At A^3 there are some rather dissonant voicings occurring on beats 3 and 4 of the 1st and 2nd measures, then parallel movement to harmonize the melody in the third measure. The note a minor 2nd above the lowest one is the dissonant tone. Entire phrases can be harmonized this way, to create a fresh and surprising sound.

Two measures before the end notice the E chord prior to the final resolution on E-flat. This harmonic device is one you can easily incorporate in a variety of tunes.

Memories of You

Andy Razaf
and Eubie Blake

Moderately slow

Wak-ing skies at sun-rise, ev-'ry sun-set too

seems to be bring-ing me Mem-o-ries Of You.

Here and there, ev-'ry-where, scenes that we once knew,

and they all just re-call Mem-o-ries Of You.

How I wish I could for-get those hap-py yes-ter-years

that have left a ro-sa-ry of tears.

Your face beams in my dreams 'spite of all I do.

Ev-'ry-thing seems to bring Mem-o-ries Of You. You.

Memories of You

Andy Razaf and Eubie Blake

61

Notes on. . .
My Melancholy Baby

This old tune has been the butt of many jokes over the years, but it's really a great classic. I found it wonderful reharmonization material.

The first measure shows an example of parallel harmonies, with the right hand using doubled octaves, and the left hand in fifths. Although this type of chord movement has been unacceptable in traditional music theory, it is very widely used in jazz and popular playing.

Note the moving alto voice in measure 6 and the 2 measure harmonic fillers in measures 7 and 8. (Look for others throughout the piece.)

The first measure of B is an example of contrary motion harmony with the root descending in half steps. This bass movement continues through the next three measures.

The final three measures are a tag ending using a very common progression. Beginning on the flat 5 (A) of the home key (E-flat), the chords descend in half steps to E-flat. Analyze these changes and practice this ending in all keys.

My Melancholy Baby

George A. Norton and
Ernie Burnett

My Melancholy Baby

George A. Norton
and Ernie Burnett

Softly, but always moving

Notes on. . .

A Nightingale Sang in Berkeley Square

All three "A" sections of this arrangement have been harmonized and styled differently, to offer you various possibilities. Watch for different types of left hand movement, inner voices and fillers as you go along.

Note the moving left hand line in measures 1, 2, and 4. This changes to a pedal point on B-flat, in measures 5 and 6, with close right hand harmonies above it. In 9 and 10 there is a filler, leading into the next section. Another one occurs two measures before the key change. This one makes use of open parallel harmonies and eighth note triads in the right hand . . . à la Bill Evans. See if you can incorporate these kinds of fillers into the other tunes you play.

At B (the bridge), the tune moves into a stride-like feeling for four measures, then back into the ballad feel until the end.

The final chord is arrived at chromatically, beginning on D-flat, a whole step below the home key, moving up to D, and finally resolving on E-flat.

A Nightingale Sang in Berkeley Square

eric Maschwitz and Manning Sherwin

Eric Maschwitz
and Manning Sherwin

Slowly

E♭maj7 Cm7 Gm7 E♭7 A♭ G7 Cm7 A♭m6

That cer-tain night, the night we met there was ma-gic a-broad in the air, there were
strange it was, how sweet and strange. There was nev-er a dream to com-pare with that

E♭maj7 B♭7 E♭7 A♭m7 D♭7 E♭maj7 Cm7 Fm7 B♭7 E♭6 Cm7

an-gels din-ing at the Ritz, and A } Night-in-gale Sang In Ber-k'ley Square.
ha-zy, cra-zy night we met, when A }

Fm7 B♭7 E♭maj7 Cm7 Gm7 E♭7 A♭maj7 G7 Cm7 A♭m6

{ I may be right, I may be wrong, but I'm per-fect-ly will-ing to swear that
This heart of mine beats loud and fast like a mer-ry-go-round in a fair. For

E♭maj7 B♭7 E♭7 A♭m7 D♭7 E♭maj7 Cm7 Fm7 B♭7 E♭6 Cm7 Cm7/B♭

when you turn'd and smiled at me A } Night-in-gale Sang In Ber-k'ley Square.
we were danc-ing cheek to cheek and A }

Am7♭5 D7 G Em7 Am7 D7 D7/C Bm7 B♭dim7 Am7 D7

{ The moon that lin-gered o-ver Lon-don town,___ poor puz-zled moon, he wore a frown.
When dawn came steal-ing up all gold and blue___ to in-ter-rupt our ren-dez-vous,

G Em7 Am7 D7 D7/C Bm7 B♭dim7 Fm7 B♭7

How could he know we two were so in love.___ The whole darn world seemed up-side down, the
I still re-mem-ber how you smiled and said,___ "Was that a dream or was it true?" Our

E♭maj7 Cm7 Gm7 E♭7 A♭ G7 Cm A♭m6 E♭ B♭7

streets of town were paved with stars. It was such a ro-man-tic af-fair, and as we kiss'd and
home-ward step was just as light as the tap-danc-ing feet of As-taire and like an e-cho

E♭7 A♭m7 D♭7 E♭ Cm7 Fm7 B♭7 |1. E♭ Cm7 Fm7 B♭7 ||2. E♭ Cm7

said "good-night" } A Night-in-gale Sang In Ber-k'ley Square.___ How Square.
far a-way }

Fm7 B♭7 B♭7/A♭ Gm7♭5 C7 Fm7♭5 A♭/B♭ B♭7 E♭ Cm Cm7/B♭ A♭m6 E♭6

I know, 'cause I was there that night in Ber-k'ley Square.___

Copyright © MCMXL The Peter Maurice Music Co., Ltd. London, England. Renewed.
Sole Selling Agent for USA/Canada: Shapiro, Bernstein & Co., Inc.
Used By Permission.

69

A Nightingale Sang in Berkeley Square

(for Stuart Isacoff)

Eric Maschwitz and
Manning Sherwin

Notes on. . .
The Star-Spangled Banner

The first reharmonization I ever heard of this piece was the lovely arrangement by John Clayton Jr., written for vocalist Whitney Houston and performed at Superbowl XXV. If you've never heard it, your ears are in for a harmonic treat!!

I began this version with simple right hand harmonies and a flowing arpeggiated left hand. The second phrase is harmonized differently, beginning with chromatically ascending voicings in measures 9 and 10. Measures 13-18 make use of descending chord roots. In measure 18, the entire quality of the chord is changed by the movement of the inner right hand voices . . . . . this happens again in measure 22. (Find other places in the arrangement where this occurs and adapt the technique to your own stylings.)

Thicker voicings and a moving left hand bring this final musical phrase to a peak. The volume increases and fermatas contribute to the drama and majesty of the ending. The final chord is D-flat MAJ.9 (the flat-5 of the home key, G).

The Star-Spangled Banner

Francis Scott Key

The Star-Spangled Banner

Francis Scott Key
and John Stafford Smith

Moderately

Oh!___ say can you see   by the dawn's ear - ly

light,   What so proud - ly we hailed   at the twi - light's last

air, Gave proof through the night that our flag was still

there. Oh! say does that star-span-gled ban - ner yet wave O'er the

cresc.

land of the free, and the home of the brave.

ff *rit.*

Notes on. . .
Ode to Joy

The first chorus of this piece begins with the melody harmonized in sixths, over a left hand pedal point on G. Note the movement of the inner voices in measures 11 and 12. This style is like that of a church organ or choral piece.

The second page begins the embellishment and reharmonization of the theme. Compare the chord changes to those in the first chorus. Notice the moving inner voices in the 1st, 7th, and 9th measures, and the gospel-like cadence on beats 3 and 4 of measure 8.

The melody in measures 9-12 of page two is harmonized over a chromatically descending bass line.

Remember to play "straight" eight notes in the last 6 measures, before cadencing on the flat 5 (D-flat) of the home key (G).

Ode to Joy

Ludwig van Beethoven

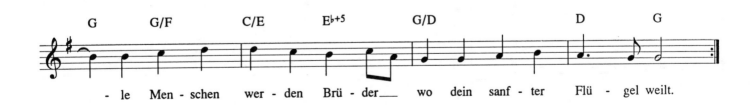

Ode to Joy

Ludwig van Beethoven

Notes on...
Prelude

This famous Chopin Prelude was originally in the key of A Major. I elected to transpose it down a whole step (G), to achieve a mellower sound. If you want to be really adventurous, transpose it back to the original key and compare the sound.

The piece opens with a left hand D pedal point, for the first seven measures. Note the movement of the inner voices in the right hand chords in this section.

In measures 11 and 12, the melody is given added strength by doubling at the octave.

Examine the left hand arpeggiated figures throughout the arrangement, remembering to play the eighth notes "straight."

At measure 17, the piece is further reharmonized, incorporating more rhythmic movement. Compare these chord changes to the original version.

The arrangement ends on the chord G/F. We can also call this F9(#11,13).

Prelude in A Major
Op. 28, No. 7

Frédéric Chopin

Andantino

Prelude

Frederic Chopin

Notes on. . .
Santa Lucia

The first chorus of this traditional tune features the melody harmonized in triads, then sixths, while being continuously supported by the arpeggiated left hand. Many of Chopin's pieces have such a bass pattern. Practice it alone first, finding comfortable fingerings to maintain the flow and steadiness of the line.

The reharmonization begins at measure 17, evolving into more complex jazz harmonies. Note the use of moving inner voices and fillers in measures 25-28.

The piece ends on D-flat . . . a half step above the home key (C).

Santa Lucia

Teodoro Cottrau

Santa Lucia

Teodoro Cottrau

Notes on. . .
(We Are) One in the Spirit

I learned this traditional tune in Sunday School, as a child. The leadsheet is in the original 4/4 meter. I have adapted it for my trio in 3/4 and it worked well enough, that we ended up recording it. The left hand features an ostinato that continues throughout the piece. The eighth notes should have a flowing swing feel and forward momentum.

In the first chorus, the right hand is voiced in perfect fourths, with the melody on top. The second chorus (beginning at measure 31) is a reharmonization, using typical jazz waltz figures, and more complex chord voicings. The left-hand ostinato re-enters for the repeated vamp in measures 51-52. Repeat this as desired, while improvising in the right hand, before continuing on to the end.

(We Are) One in the Spirit

Traditional

(We Are) One in the Spirit

Traditional

93

Notes on. . .
Wild Rose

This is a lovely piece I first became familiar with in junior high school . . . through my clarinet lessons. There is a wonderful recording of it, by Sonny Rollins, that I highly recommend.

Of all the arrangements in the book, this one is the most personal and emotional for me. Influences from favorite composers are woven into various measures. In the first four measures of A, Erik Satie and his Gymnopedies come to mind. Australian composer/pianist, Percy Grainger's harmonies are reflected in measures 3 and 4 of B, and shades of Debussy can be heard in measures 5-8 of that same section.

At D, the reharmonization and voicings create a whole new sound, mood and thought, following the ritard in the previous two measures. Measures 4-6 of E illustrate harmonies over a chromatically descending bass line.

Note the left hand arpeggios throughout the piece. These should remain a gentle and flowing support to the melodic line, which has been harmonized mostly by open intervals and triads.

The last six measures involve two ritards, and should be played as expressively as possible, to the harmonically simple end.

To a Wild Rose

Edward MacDowell

Wild Rose

Dedicated To Michael A. Grey
(1957-1991)

Edward MacDowell

99